A Trip To Far Away Beach

By Ranaja Mitchell & Chief Melendez

Inspired by our family & friends at Case Prep & the Maple Valley Branch Library in Akron Ohio.

At circle time, Elle and Chief listen to a story about boat's .

It's time for a snack! Chief brought a banana. Elle brought a bagel. Christian brought a beef patty and Zhyeon brought broccoli.

During quite time Chief reads a book about the beach.

He falls asleep during the story and begins to dream.

He dreams of a beach far far away.

He sees himself sitting in the Sand. Smiling back at the hot sun.

He heads towards the trees and look who he sees! It's Zhyeon relaxing in the breeze.

They wave hello. Chief asks Zhyeon if he'd like to explore the beach! And off they go.

They arrived to the shore and look who they see! It's Christian with a big whale!

They wave hello! Elle invites them to join her on the beach. And off the go!

They began to play and enjoy the day!

Together they played soccer.

It's Ms.Felicia! She asks Chief to wake up because quite time is over.

While Ms.Felicia collects the books around the class. Chief tells her about his dream.

It was a wonderful day! Class is done! Now it's time to go home and play!

Made in the USA
Middletown, DE
24 March 2023